Nowadays, beetles in Brazil are bright green and gold. But in the beginning, they were all dull and brown. This is the story of how the beetle got her bright green-gold coat.

One day long ago in Brazil, a little brown beetle was walking up the side of a high wall. The beetle was walking slowly because she only had little legs.

Suddenly, a big rat popped out from a hole in the wall.

"You are so slow," said the rat, rudely. "Look at me, and see how quickly I can run!"

With that, the rat scampered up to the top of the wall and then back to the beetle. He was very speedy. But he was quite mean and boastful, too.

"You are very quick indeed," said the beetle, who was very polite.

"I bet you would like to run as speedily as me," said the rat.

"Maybe so," said the beetle politely.

A bright green-gold parrot was sitting on top of the wall, listening to the beetle and the rat.

“We should have a contest,” said the parrot.

“Yes,” said the tailor bird, who was sitting next to the parrot.

"To make things interesting," the tailor bird went on, "I will make a bright new coat for whichever of you gets from here to... that mango tree first."

And the tailor bird pointed with her wing to a tree high up on top of a mountain.

"How would you like your coat to look if you win?" said the tailor bird to the rat and the beetle.

"I will definitely win this," said the rat. "And I want a yellow coat with black stripes, like a tiger's."

The beetle looked at the green-gold parrot, the green-gold mango in the tree, the green hills and the golden sunshine.

"I would like a green and gold coat, please," said the beetle.

The rat giggled.

"You will not beat me!" he boasted.

"We shall see who wins," said the two birds.

So the rat and the beetle lined up at the starting point.

"Ready, steady, go!" said the parrot.

Then she and the tailor bird flew up to the mango tree on the mountain so that they could see who got there first.

At first, the big rat ran as quickly as he could, but then he slowed down.

"What is the point of rushing?" he said to himself. "I will win anyway."

So the rat took his time. He crawled up the cliff, resting whenever he felt tired. But when he reached the tree at the top of the mountain, he was surprised to see that the beetle had gotten there before him!

“You must have cheated,” said the rat to the beetle. “How could you have beaten me? You are so slow.”

“No one said I had to run,” said the beetle, “so I flew instead.”

With that, the little brown beetle lifted up her wing cases and showed off her little wings.

"I never knew you could fly!" said the rat.

"You should never underestimate anyone," said the parrot.

So the rat lost the contest. As a result, even in Brazil, where the flowers, animals, and insects are all bright, the rat still has a dull coat.

Then the birds turned to the beetle.

"Here is your green and gold coat," said the tailor bird.

The beetle put on the bright new coat. It fitted her perfectly. From that day on, beetles in Brazil have had bright green-gold coats.